Herbert the Mouse

An Epic of Gorthon

Written by M. J. Gusk

Illustrations by Carter Bastin

To order additional copies of this book, contact:
Xlibris
844-714-8691
www.Xlibris.com
Orders@Xlibris.com

ISBN: Softcover   979-8-3694-3040-8
         EBook   979-8-3694-3041-5

Library of Congress Control Number: 2024920033

Print information available on the last page

Rev. date: 12/17/2024

Acknowledgements

Thank you to Mrs. Fox my old English teacher for starting me on this journey.
Thank you to my mom for believing in me.
Thank you to Carter for bringing my world visually to life.
Lastly, thank you dear reader for reading my story.
I hope you enjoy it as much as I had writing it all these years.

The City of Daron is Abandoned
Thus, it has been this way for thirty years. The only true inhabitant who still
holds his bearings is a mouse named Herbert. Yet destiny has yet to play its final
hand in the life of Herbert as he is set to one simple and life-changing quest.
To find a suitable person to become king and restore the kingdom to its glory.
The fate of Southan lies with one mouse, and a boy.

Table of Contents

Chapter One:

HERBERT THE MOUSE

'Thirty years, it has been.' thought the mouse as he was making his way around the castle's keep. Pattering his way through several holes, and cracks. 'Thirty years since that cursed elf came into our kingdom and ruined it, ruined everything.' Herbert, as the mouse was named, thought back to when the keep had been a hub of activity and grandeur. A kingdom to rival that of their northern neighbors, the kingdom of Than-In. During that time, they had been visited by an elf in dark robes who promised them riches and rewards. He promised to make the king a great man amongst all. For days, that elf had stayed with them in feast and merry making. Yet disaster came upon them the third day when the tragedy struck. The elf tricked the king and cursed him and addled his mind, as he had long been an ally to the king of Than-In. He killed all the king's sons, daughters, and all his lords.

He turned the king mad and fled the castle. For many years the kingdom had not seen aid until five years ago hearing word that Meradoth had been defeated, and the Kingdom of the North now ruled by one called Gregory, who sent supplies to the needy of the kingdom. But now the aid had stopped as a drought was occurring in all the lands, and the people were starving. This was going to be a long winter when it came, and many would die. Herbert breathed deeply in thought as he reached the grand hall, whereas always the king was sitting on his throne. His hair had long since grown out, only being trimmed by the mouse on rare occasions, and he was attempting to call council. Looking around the room, however, made it clear that no such council would be held. The seats of all the lords and ladies that once held them were in ruin, either by age, or destroyed. Bones from those who were on this once great council lay dusty and broken. Herbert had walked in right as the king was attempting something of a roll call.

"Lord Ashford, where is Lord Ashford?"

Gazing around the empty room the derelict king nodded. Having seemed to have assured himself of his inane reasoning.

"Late again, that's the fifth time this year, I'll have to send a raven to his keep."

Little did the crazed king notice, but the bones of the previous Lord Ashford had been only twenty feet away right at the spot he had died protecting the king that fateful day. This carried on for some time; Herbert adopted a perch high above in the rafters and frowned. 'Master, I wish there was something I could do for you, but I am just a humble pet mouse.' He turned tail not long after and made his way out of the keep and into the city for which the keep was located. The City of Daron they had called it, but now a common short-handed name for it was now known as the barren city. Nothing had lived in the city since that fateful day. Making his way across the drawbridge as it creaked and groaned under him. Looking down into the moat, he wondered if anything lived in the water. He shook his head and threw that from his mind. If anything did live down there it was most likely able to eat him, and that was not something to think about.

Making his way into the city, one could tell that it was once a glorious, and a very lively place. Now the streets echoed with the sounds of alley cats, and dogs, or the occasional rat. The only things that could survive such a place. The cracked windows and broken buildings made him shudder; they always did. He slowly made his way to the hill near town, there was a rock there he liked to perch on and watch the fields flow and look at the landscape. 'This was a fine city, now it's a dead husk.'

Making his way up the hill as the sun was rising to midday. The mouse was smiling, if you could tell a smile on a mouse. He enjoyed the view, and it made him appreciate the larger world. The golden wheat fields blew in the gentle breeze, soon it would be harvesting season, and winter would come as it had come every time before. For now, though he enjoyed the view. Behind him a glowing light had come not from the sun, but from somewhere below it. It was near blinding to the mouse; he ran behind the rock where he could afford some safety. The light glowed brighter until it suddenly stopped, and where the glow had come a person had stood, someone that had not been there before. He looked elderly, yet unlike many of those folk held himself high in regards. A long white beard, and a white cloak barred him from the world. In his hand, a large staff made of some wood, of ash or willow. The mouse breathed not knowing what to do; he could make it away unseen; he was small enough. Yet just as the thought crossed his mind, the voice of the figure called out.

"And where are you running off to my friend?"

Herbert froze, 'he cannot have been talking to me,' thought the mouse. He crept forward a few paces, when the voice called again.

"I AM talking to you, my young mouse friend, why don't you come back and come atop the rock so I may see you."

The mouse, in fear, wondered if the distant voice could read a creatures' mind. Herbert, though hesitant, trusted the voice, and the figure who carried it. He slowly approached the rock, though willing to dash at the first sign of trouble. With minimal effort, he reached the top of the rock and looked into the face of the man. The figure held a large nose, and long white hair. His face, though wrinkled, looked strangely young, and youthful for a figure that Herbert had to have put in his late eighties.

"There you are my small friend, and I do say you've kept yourself well taken care of since your masters' fall from sanity."

Herbert looked at the stranger, he had no doubt that the stranger knew of his master, but how had he known that the king was his master. The stranger looked at the mouse and smiled.

"Oh my young Herbert, you've seen better days. What if I told you I could give them back to you?"

Herbert's heart almost skipped a beat, was this man who had come from the light going to give him back his master? Was he finally going to restore his masters' twisted mind?'

The figure as though reading the thoughts of Herbert frowned, his face creased.

"I am sorry, but I can't restore what has happened to your master. There is one thing I can do though, if you'll allow it?" Herbert's heart sank, the brief glimmer of hope had been dashed, but he would hear the stranger out.

"What has happened to your master was of his own design, he may have not asked for it but allowing it to happen is just the same. I can't restore his mind, but I can give you a new king, but this task is one you must endeavor on your own."

Herbert was confused; you had to be of some grand house or have the blood of the king in you. No ordinary man would be king, no one would take it. He had never heard of such a thing happening. Herbert was confused also by having himself do it, he was a mouse after all, and mice cannot elect kings. The stranger seemed to know all of this and answered.

"I can help you; I can give you the gift of voice, and you will use this power to find the next king. Once this task is done, bring him to this hill, and I will crown him. Your kingdom will have a new king and you a new master."

Herbert stood what would be in shock at the request. The gift of voice why he deserved this gift, and who was this man to give it. He had heard rumors of men of magic powers able to give strange gifts, but this was something very different. Also, what authority gave this being the ability to crown a new king at will, what will he do if he has to give such power to others. The stranger, as though in response, sat down and came close to the mouse.

"Do you know who I am, my little friend?"

The mouse frowned and shook his head.

"Look deep within, and you will see."

Herbert couldn't tell what he meant, but he focused on the stranger, and suddenly an overpower of some sort came over him, and the one thing that came to him was the creator, this stranger was THE creator. In response, the old man moved his magical staff in a circle motion. As though summoning clouds or waving the air he held a dim light at its tip and touched the throat of the mouse. Herbert smiled, he finally understood eons of memories and lives flowed through him at once as though he had lived a thousand lifetimes.

All the way back to the beginning, "Istan, your Istan my old friend." The mouse dipped his head as the being smiled once again.

"Hello Herbert, it is nice to see you again."

Herbert was somewhat confused; he looked around not only at himself, but his new surroundings.

"Again, what do you mean?"

Istan grabbed the mouse and held him in the palm of his hand, "You are awakened, as you were when I met you back then you called me the Wanderer."

The mouse who at first looked confused, suddenly gave the look of mesmerism.

"I remember," Herbert looked around, though he was not the same mouse he was a moment ago. "This place has changed much since we roamed it all those eons ago hasn't it."

Istan smiled, "Indeed my old friend, now to the task at hand, can you accomplish such a task?" The mouse climbed onto the shoulder of the great being, "You wouldn't have brought me back if I wouldn't be able to Istan. I will find the next king."

Istan got up and moved the mouse from his shoulder and back onto the rock.

"Good, it has been so wonderful to see you my friend, but I must be off. Please be quick, the days grow shorter and colder. The last wrong must be righted. Farewell, for now."

With that the being vanished off into a cascade of light and was gone. Herbert was alone, and when he looked around the sun was already halfway to its afternoon cycle.

"I have spent too much time away; I must return with haste."

Running on all fours, he made a dash for the keep. There was much to be done, before he could depart.

Chapter Two:
THE SEARCH BEGINS

Herbert went back to the castle and made his way back into the keep. Making his way into what was once the keeps' kitchen. Once several servants had worked and labored in this room; now it stood as a room for the mouse, though being a mouse, he did not need much room. In the corner closest to the old furnace.

"This old room may finally have people in it one day."

He made a small mouse-like smile. Cheerful thoughts raced through his mind. Gathering what little mouse things he needed he set up a small kit out of an old pouch he had taken from one the dead lords, and used it for his own uses, in this case it would serve as his travel pack. After taking the rest of the afternoon to gather the rest of his things. The sun was going to set soon, and Herbert decided to head out the next morning. That night a large storm hit the castle and blew old boards off the hinges and broke others apart. But the storm ended as all others have, and the morning promised to be a wet one, the travel would be hard going, with the promise of better days ahead. As the evening clouds of rain and mist parted as the sun rose and made way for the dawn that was when Herbert awoke from his sleep. His master was quiet as ever, of course he hadn't eaten since his mind alteration, he hadn't needed to, something that happened that day had stopped his body and hung him in a state of undeath. He neither aged, nor did he starve; he just kept up living. Herbert, however, was not so, and ate a small morning meal, before getting ready to start his journey.

Before he left, he visited his master, even after all these years he still loved his master.

"Don't worry master," he said in his mouse-like voice.

"One day I'll return, and I'll save you I promise."

The only response he received was a wild response from his master, who thought that one of his lords had spoken to him, something about sending troops to the eastern border.

"Don't give up, master, I'll return, you'll see."

He left not long after and soon he was making his way out of the city, and into the wild Fields of Panadore. The day for the mouse was uneventful and he always tried getting to as high of a place as possible in order to get an idea as to where he was. Though he was only a mouse he was very intelligent and had studied the map of his masters' kingdoms many times. He knew the lands very well, and even when he didn't have the gift of speech, he would tell himself strategies and war plans that the lords his master listened to would never hear and would never have thought of. He didn't think he was better than those his master took to console but he thought that even the opinions of his should be heard by all. As he climbed the cliff he was on, the clouds came closer as though he could touch the sky. After reaching a shelf on the cliff face, he rested and looked out onto the landscape in front of him. He saw more than he had ever seen before. This was what his master had ruled over this large expanse of land that seemed to go from horizon to horizon. Looking up Herbert could see that the sun was setting over the distant hills. Herbert looked around; though he had been following the road he must have traveled further than he thought. The mouse decided to try his best to find a small nook and sleep for the night. Soon thereafter he found it at the base of an oak tree set a few feet into the tree line. Curling up into a ball, he shifted about and finally found his comfort spot. The mouse soon drifted off into sleep, as the moon rose high into the sky.

Later that night it was Herbert's instinctual senses that awoke him from his slumber. He dashed from his sleeping spot just in time as he heard the hiss of a serpent nearby and it banged into his sleeping hole. 'Snakes,' the mouse thought as he pulled out his impromptu blade and gave it a small flourish. 'I hate snakes.' Now Herbert never had to deal with them at the palace but whenever he traveled outside of the city, he always made sure to be mindful of them. Herbert cursed; he had been so focused on his quest he had forgotten one of his basic reminders. The snake curled itself out of the nook and once again faced the mouse. It opens its mouth, its large, curled fangs facing the house mouse. Herbert braced himself and readied for the incoming strike, the serpent came with its mighty lunge with the mouse just narrowly escaping its pounce. The serpent, having expected the mouse to pull a trick, whirled around but not before Herbert swung widely at his opponent striking the snake on its scaly hide. Blood shot out from the wound and sprayed across the two opponents. Herbert knew he had to think of something quick, or he would lose the fight. Snakes have more energy, and body mass to rely on than the poor house mouse. Herbert looked to the tree while the snake was taking its own time, careful not to undertake the mouse that bit back. Herbert saw an opportunity, there was a dead branch that had fallen and mingled with another roughly ten feet up, it was pointy and might do the trick. First, he had to break the other branches that held it in place. So, the mouse jumped and just in time as the serpent had lunged at him just as he clung onto its lowest branches, luckily for the mouse this knocked one of the smaller twig-like branches off and lightly hit the snake making shuffles backwards right to where Herbert wanted him. Herbert got the place he intended just above the branch and began to jump up and down.

"This is for waking me up, you foul creature."

At his final word, the twig that was really holding the branch came down, and so did it fell, with a thud, and large hiss. Herbert saw his opponent slither off leaving a trail of blood behind it. Herbert firmly nodded and climbed back down the tree. The mouse was smiling, and a ray of light hit him. It had been closer to morning than he had originally thought. Herbert struck his blade into the ground at the base of the tree and rubbed off his hands in triumph and smugness. Who would blame the mouse? There weren't many stories of little mice doing brave feats as such as he had done. The mouse walked to the edge of the cliff where the road took a sudden turn and went downward into a small valley. There in the far middle of a field he saw small clouds of smoke rising in the open plain. There seemed to be a town, if his memory was correct this was most likely the town of Buran, a larger city about twenty miles east of the capital.

"That should be my first stop; hopefully I can end this quest sooner than later."

Herbert looked at himself and decided that he had earned some rest. Thinking more carefully about his resting spot, he slept for a small number of hours. Herbert awoke with no snakes to interpret him this time. After he rose and stretched out, he went back down the road and made his way towards Buran. The sun was already lowering into the midday sky by the time he got into the city.

It was alive with activity, and many people were still up and about. Many were common peasants, and farmers. They were buying their supplies for the day or getting new tools in readiness for the harvest season. Herbert was going to speak, but he had the notion that he probably shouldn't talk to the people, not until he found the one who would be the new king. As this thought came to mind, he remembered that he hadn't even been told who to look for. Istan didn't tell him who to look for. Herbert immediately ran into a nearby alleyway, he had been hovering close to anyway, but this was something different entirely. His heart was racing at what felt like the speed of charging horses. His breath was short, and his mind raced. Why hadn't Istan told him who it was? Finding a person who he knew the name of was easier than finding someone he had no name for at all.

"Istan, you never gave me a sign, now I'm out in the far world and I could really use a sign now." As though Istan or even the heavens above had heard his plea a small voice called out to him. It seemed to have belonged to a young boy, he guessed in his middle youthful years.

"Hello, what's a poor little mouse like you doing here?"

Herbert turned and saw that the young man was dressed in a gray tunic, and dark pants. He wore a large hat that attempted to cover up the large amount of brown hair that seemed a mess. His face had some freckles, and his eyes were a light blue. The boy was reaching out as though to grab him, or some form of introduction. Herbert cautiously approached, knowing that if there was any trouble he would dash away as soon as possible.

"Hello there little guy, you look worn out, why don't you come home with me?"

Herbert was going to speak, but he did not want to talk to the boy, and especially not in public. He nodded, and the boy scooped him into a pocket in his tunic.

"It's nice to have a friend, my name is Kregar, son of Dregar. Do you have a name, little guy?" The mouse nodded, or what he would think a nod was. The boy seemed to understand.

"Oh well you probably have a master, don't you?"

The mouse nodded again; the boy looked sad but tried his best to hide it.

"Is he close by?"

The mouse shook his head, "Oh he's far away?"

The mouse nodded and tried indicating a general direction.

"That way but the only thing that way is the old castle. I've never seen it, but they say our king lives there. Is your master from the old castle?"

Herbert nodded, the boy's expression turned from a frown, to what could only be described as wonderment.

"Who are you little one? You know you're far from home, why don't I look after you. Don't worry, you'll be safe. My parents own a farm outside of town. I'll take you there."

Herbert nodded, 'Finally,' he thought some form of civilization was better than staying out in the wilderness, which he had not been looking forward to. It was only a matter of roughly a quarter sundial when they arrived at the boys' farm. It was a decent sized estate, which held the house, the stables, and a few small sheds, which most likely held the tools and gear needed from such tasks. Behind all this was a vast field that went on for some distance. Whoever this Kregar, son of Dregar was, his family was very well off for themselves. The house was very modest, and held only what room those needed, farmers were simple folk. Entering the house he immediately came upon the pair was the smell of something cooking in another room.

"Mother, father I'm home," called the boy out into the house.

A head suddenly came out from behind a wall that divided the entrance and sitting room from the kitchen. It was an older woman, who seemed very cheerful, whose hair matched Kregar's own.

"Oh Kregar, how did the shopping go? Did you get a good deal from that crook Negan?"

Kregar walked into the kitchen and put down the sack he was holding, "It wasn't the worst deal he gave us, but I swear his prices go up every time."

Kregar's mother grabbed the items in the bag, which consisted of two loaves of bread, and lots of vegetables, as well as a covered meat case.

"Well, he may be a crook, but he's not the only one, stories are going around that this drought won't be ending soon. That rain last night was good for the crops, but it won't be enough." Herbert could see tears forming at the edges of her eyes.

"Don't worry Kregar, why don't you get changed, and clean yourself up, supper will be ready soon and your father will be back out from the fields soon. Go on."

Kregar went into a room that had a bed, and many chests and cabinets in it.

"This is my room, little one, you can wait here until I get back. I'm going to get cleaned up." Kregar set Herbert down on the bed, which was very comfy to the mouse. He watched as the boy gathered a few articles of clothing and made his way down the hallway and into a room, where the sounds of a water pump could be heard.

"So that's the washroom," Herbert said aloud.

He made his way over to the windowsill, which was a nice small window. Out of it, he could see the barn and the fields beyond. He saw a large man, in similar clothes as his son; enter the building with a cart hauled by a mule behind him. He was giving snacks and petting it. It must have been a hard day at work for the farmer.

As he was looking out the window a memory he had long since forgotten came back to him, it was when he was a young mouse, and his master, and then a prince had found him abandoned in the alleyways near the castle.

"Hello there little guy? What are you doing out here? Here, why don't I take you home with me?" The memory left him just as soon as it had come.

"That was the beginning of a beautiful friendship."

Herbert smiled, and a single small mouse tear made his way down his long nose.

"My, well that's new."

Herbert watched the older farmer pack away his things and make his way towards the dwelling. As he did, he heard the footsteps of Kregar coming back from his wash. Entering the room the young man only had his trousers on, Herbert could see that the life of a farmer had muscled the young man up. Quickly putting on a light blue tunic, he smiled and made his way over to his bed, where he looked up at the ceiling.

"You know I'm happy I found you, it's nice to have someone around that isn't my parents." Hebert came over to the bed and watched the young man inquisitively. Herbert knew the feeling all too well from his own master, who had been raised up a single child and heir to the throne that he took not because he wanted to, but because it was his duty. That is why he found such companionship in Herbert and Herbert found that companionship in the prince, they were two halves of a whole.

"Kregar, come get your food dear."

His mother had called from down in the dining area.

"I'm on the way," he turned to his mouse friend.

"Don't worry, I'll save you a bit. See you later."

Once again, he left Herbert alone in his room. Herbert did not want to stay in the room, he wanted to explore. Making his way out of the room, he found himself in a long hallway that seemed to divide the house. He made his way towards what he had earlier identified as the washroom. Entering the room, he saw a large area where one would wash oneself, and another was towels or similar to towels. The room was lit with many candles, most of them were for light, and others smelled. Herbert exited the room and made his way into what was of course another bedroom. This one was a bit larger than the young man's, and the bed was also larger. There was nothing fancy about it, but Herbert was still impressed by its size. Looking around it was nearly identical in layout to Kregar's room. He left the room, and just by looking around this area of the house was the least used by the family. Which was not entirely new to the mouse; he had noticed that many mortals were away from their bedchambers while the sun was out, but when it sank, it was back into the beds. He found it curious, and hilarious in a sort of way. Making his way towards the dining and kitchen areas, he heard the older man talking most likely to his son.

"Kregar what did you do today, I was hoping to have you in the fields today."

Kregar swallowed a bite of food, before he responded, "Mother asked me to go shopping for her, as she said that I worked really hard yesterday, and earned a break."

Kregar's father laughed, and most likely clapped his son on the back in one of those father son ways.

"That you did, you threw over a dozen bales of wheat over your head and onto the pile before I could get you to stop." There was a pause as more of the meal was eaten.

"The time before that you insisted on cutting the weeds in the patch in the west field, it took you three hours, but by Mentros you did it. You did earn a break son, but I want you up good and early tomorrow for the gathering in the south fields. Come on now and eat."

The family was in silence as the sounds of food and utensils made their way to Herberts' ears. Rounding the corner, little did he know but from the way he had come the father was facing him, and it was at that time he looked up and saw Herbert slowly approaching.

"A mouse! Kregar, hand me a knife." The father ran towards Herbert, a knife from the table in hand. The middle-aged farmer began to chase Herbert who once he had seen began dashing away. The chase began in the kitchen, and Herbert made his way into Kregar's room. Kregar in turn began shouting to his father trying to get his attention.

"Father, don't hurt him, I found him!"

In turn, Dregar turned to his son who had followed him while in the chase.

"What do you mean you found him? Don't you know that more of them will show up, treat one rodent kind, and more will come. We must kill it now."

Kregar looked sad, and before Dregar could open the door a voice which was small and slightly squeaky.

"Pardon sir, but I would not rather die tonight."

Kregar, and Dregar stopped talking, so they turned to the door. Kregar opened it and saw the mouse he had found in the streets; this time he had dressed in what could only be described as a mouse version of a blue tunic and hat. The mouse was standing in the middle of the room looking at the two in the doorway.

"Now if you'll allow me, I'll explain myself."

Herbert said, now the elder man may have screamed or charged the mystical mouse, but something compelled him not to that night. Whether it was his strong will, or some sort of unseen force, Herbert never knew. Instead, the man lowered his knife and went away words mumbled under his breath.

"This world is stranger than I thought."

Herbert joined Kregar in the middle of the room who picked up the mouse in the palm of his hand.

"You can talk," said the young farmer.

Herbert nodded, "Yes, though this was a gift I was given only a day ago, and with it I can change the fate of our people."

Kregar frowned, as he guided him out of the room and into the sitting room where his mother and father sat. They were just discussing what had happened when the pair approached.

"I apologize. I did not expect that we would meet like this."

Kregar's mother almost fainted, as his father looked carefully at Herbert.

"So, what in all the fates are you?"

Kregar set Herbert down on a table in the sitting room and he looked carefully at all three of his hosts.

"My name is Herbert the Mouse, and I am a pet mouse to our King. Long ago, he was twisted and mangled by the elf Meradoth. For years, I have watched him live in the husk of life he has left. I have been given the ways of voice and have been awakened with one task to fulfill. To find a new king and save our people."

Dregar looked at the mouse and he faced a mixture of disbelief and curiosity.

"So, you didn't always talk?" said Dregar's wife; whose name Herbert never found out.

Herbert smiled at the farm wife.

"No, my lady I did not, this gift was given to me just at midday yesterday."

The family looked at the mouse and gave strange looks.

"So did your gift giver tell you who this new king would be?"

Herbert frowned, "I am afraid not, but I have taken my own intuition on the matter and if that is the case I am to find someone who treated me like my own master once did."

The farmer looked at his wife, and then back to the mouse.

"Now I do not know who your master was like, or what he is like, so I cannot help you. We cannot help you."

The mouse shook his head, "You can think my lord, I was thinking of this when I was alone in your sons' room. My master found me on the streets and took me in. and treated me nicely, and with compassion were as many in the castle would have seen me killed. After years, me and him became nearly inseparable. We grew a bond, and when your son found me in the market alleyway today, I saw the same type of spark in him."

The farmer, though not a fully learned man, was able to understand what the mouse was saying, "Are you saying that you think my son," he pointed at his son to make his point clear.

"You think he is worthy to be a king, not just any king but our king?"

Herbert looked over at Kregar and smiled at the young man, who returned the gesture.

"Yes, my lord farmer, I do. If a man can look at a mouse such as myself with compassion and trust. Imagine what he would do for his people. I think Kregar has earned my respect, and if that is all it takes to be king then he has what it takes."

Dregar laughed, and sat down; his laughter would die down, as he looked between the mouse and his son.

"You think that because my son took you in, that makes him a king? Half the boys in the kingdom would do the same thing, what makes my son any different from all those others?" Herbert looked at the man, and to his wife.

"You are right, his age might do the same, but when your son found me in the alleyways today, I saw something in him, care, and humanity. Something I haven't seen in over twenty years. Maybe he's young, maybe he's brash, maybe his winters are too few, maybe his youthful behavior calls, call it what you will sir. I see a young man who can grow up and be a great one. I was charged to find a new king like my master of old, and in your son, I have found just that. What do you say?"

He wasn't looking at Dregar, but his wife.

"My son is young, foolish, and simple of mind. But he is also kind, and willing. He looks after those others would not, he cares where others do not. My son is many things, and if he thinks he is a worthy young mouse lord, he could be your king. The voice she spoke in was soft and tender. "Tell me my mouse guest," began Dregar, who had a rough and bitter tone about him.

"Even if you think he is right to be, what about this person who awakened you? What would they say? And what about us? I plan on giving this land to my son before I die, what would you have us do?"

The mouse climbed up and onto the house's fireplace. He looked over his three hosts carefully.

"I shall give you a fortnight. I will have all of you decide, I shall live in the barn and shall not interrupt your daily affairs. By the end of such time. I will require an answer, and maybe I can see more of your son and who he is as a person."

The family looked at one another and Dreger nodded, rising slowly from his chair.

"Alright our mouse friend you have yourself a deal. We shall meet again in one fortnight. Until then, I am very tired, and this night has been filled with many strange tales. I shall retire, goodnight."

The rest of the family joined him slowly afterwards, until at last it was just Herbert and Kregar. "Do you really think I can be a king?"

Herbert was on his outside to the barn and had made it to the dwelling's doorway before he answered.

"I believe so, but it's not my decision, it's yours. What do you want young Kregar, what is the life you want?"

Herbert went outside before Kregar could respond, and Kregar went to bed that night with his mind a whirlwind. Herbert found a small pile of hay, and made a small nook, and went to sleep, he knew he was right, he just had to show Kregar he was right.

That night a white figure came down and approached the farmhouse in the dark. The figure came to the door and made it into the house. Entering the room of Kregar the figure waved his hands over the young man and whispered into his ear.

"You are worthy to go to the town square tomorrow, at midday, and all will see why you will be king."

The figure vanished out of the room as Kregar stirred in his sleep and was seen outside the barn. "Don't worry my old friend, you will see you have made the right choice, all of your kingdom will see why the farm boy will be king."

The figure vanished as the moon light shone over it, and was not seen again that night, or any other night since.

Chapter Three:
A BOY NAMED KREGAR

The next day the family awoke and was eating breakfast when suddenly Kregar announced his daily plans to his family.

Dregar was not impressed, "What do you mean you have to go to the city square by midday you're supposed to help me in the fields remember."

Herbert had woken up before dawn had fully risen and was watching the morning rituals of the family. The first rays of light had just hit the earth.

"I know, father. I just feel compelled, as though something is telling me to go there today." Dreger looked at his son, a look of bewilderment across his face.

"Why son, what has gotten into, is it because of last night? Has this whole idea of being a king gotten to your head already?"

Kregar ate his meal. He couldn't describe why, but it's like a sort of fate was telling him to go there, he had to. Later at around midmorning he and his father were getting their animals ready for their work in the field that day when Herbert came around the corner.

"Good morning, my lords."

The farmer at most ignored him but nodded his head.

"Good morning, Herbert, any plans today?"

Herbert was crawling up the rafters, and onto the hay bale, he had slept on last night.

"Not really, I was planning on napping today, maybe doing some exploring. This is my first time out in the wider world, you know."

Herbert was smiling at the pair before vanishing to the second floor of the barn, and the only thing Kregar heard was the squeaking of the mouse.

"Come on Kregar, let's go and start gathering the southern field."

Kregar walked out of the barn, and followed his father; Herbert looked out the window watching the pair walking out into the winding vast fields.

Herbert looked around, "I think I will head into town. I have an entire fortnight after all, might as well get to know the town while I am here."

With that notion, he made his back down onto the ground and began the journey into town.

In the field, Kregar was hard at work, the sun was warm today, and the sky was cloudless. Sweat had already started dripping from his head and onto his clothes, and mostly dry ground. Though they had rain, it was not enough. Most of the plants were dying; many of the old folks in town who couldn't work anymore were saying that they were cursed. Kregar tried not to listen to them, his father had said that it was just a bit of bad luck. Kregar's family had been farmers for as long as you could trace their lineage, which according to his parents could be traced all the way back to when this land was first settled over three hundred years ago. As he was working the working father son pair were being separated by more and more land until about a good barn length separated them. As the sun according to the sundial nearby was approaching noon,

Kregar was looking about. Even though it was a hot day, he had suddenly felt a chill reach him and go throughout his entire body.

"What on Gorthon was that?"

His father was still far away, focusing on his work. Kregar looked towards the house; nothing to be seen. He gazed around the farmlands; nothing. At last, he looked towards the barn, and there he saw it. Or whatever it was. Kregar saw a white figure who seemed to not be there. The figure didn't seem to touch the ground, and sort of hung in the air like an apparition. The figure used what could only be described as an arm, the arm pointed towards the city, and Kregar nodded, he knew that he could not ignore the call that seemed to come from deep within his mind. The apparition vanished and Kregar set down his tools, it was at this time his father was looking his way. Only to find his son on the road heading towards the town.

"Dammit boy, what are you doing?"

He slowly began to follow his son, calling to him, though it appeared that Kregar ignored him. "Kregar, where are you going?"

Suddenly Kregar began to run as though the winds had taken him. Dregar stopped at the path in front of his house. Watching his son run into town, though he didn't want to admit it, he was very proud of his son, he clenched his fist, and said to himself in an almost whisper tone, "Go on Kregar, it's your destiny claim it."

The white figure appeared behind him and smiled. They both watched as he ran down the road and vanished over the hill.

"Now your destiny has arrived, will you take it, or let it slip from your fingers?"

A ghostly white figure said, Dregar swore he heard something behind at that moment, but when he turned, nothing was there, only his wife in the doorway watching him.

"Get the cart, I have a feeling we need to go to town."

Walking towards the barn, he was smiling, like only a father who is proud of his own would smile. Their lives would be changed today whether he liked it or not.

In the town square, it was still before noon and Herbert had made his way towards the many shops and market carts that cluttered the town this time of day. Many folks were wandering to and from, making their social visits, or shopping hoping for any way to curve the growing pains of this drought. Herbert noted that because of the drought many of the market carts were low if not outright empty with foods like carrots, lettuce, corn, and beats. He was winding from one alleyway and towards another when a cry came out from the market square off to his right some ways. The call drew his attention as well as many onlookers, making his way easily through the crowd, but also making sure he wasn't stepped on when he saw what had called the cry out. On the ground, an older woman was cut bleeding from what appeared to be her arm. Her cart was in ruins, and over her a large robust man with a short blade in hand fresh with blood who stood over her in a dominating position.

"What's the problem?"

He was saying in a mocking tone that though he was responding to a quarry he might have had with her.

"You're charging three times more for your goods than you did yesterday. That is what your problem is."

She was in tears, and where he had cut she was holding tightly. She was pleading with the man, when Herbert finally arrived.

"Please just take what you want and please leave me alone."

The man didn't seem to take her pleas into consideration, but he in turn leaned in closer to an uncomfortable distance and began to say something into her ear. Herbert couldn't hear what he said, but immediately after the woman started to fight him off or at least attempt to, but it was for not. The man was much larger than herself, and her struggle only seemed to bring delight to the man, Herbert could not stand for this. Whether this lady had changed her prices on her goods did not matter, this sort of behavior he could not stand for. This was when he leaped into action. He charged from the crowd, it was only this when he remembered that though he wanted to commit to an action he couldn't do much, he was just a mouse, then a thought struck him. 'He was just a mouse, and he would do what none of these common onlookers would make this man pay for.' He quickly and cautiously approached the entangled pair, as he attempted to find a good place to grab onto, for once, the large man found out about him it would be good for the brave mouse.

He carefully grabbed onto the man's trousers, and began to make his way up, until he was able to grab onto the overly large shirt of the man. The man had not ignored this, and when he felt something grab onto him or what it felt to him, something crawling on him he began trying to brush Herbert away with his hand, while still holding onto the poor lady. As this was going on, suddenly a young man's voice reached the ears of the three members of the struggle, but also the crowd who had formed around a mixture of features, some were shocked, others growing, and yet more just watching. Yet none were doing anything to stop it, all except the little brave mouse and a boy of only fifteen or so winters under his belt, as he came charging into the crowd. It was at this moment Herbert felt the hand and felt it hit so hard it threw him off, and onto the ground, his mouth was bleeding as a result.

"What in the Pits, a mouse!"

He attempted to step on the mouse, but Herbert was just that much faster, and at that moment Kregar recognized the voice it was that disliked, but mostly kind man Negan, who was dressed like a common crook.

"Negan, what are you doing to Madame Harron?"

This caught the man off guard, and he stopped trying to crush the mouse to focus on the boy. "Kregar?"

He sounded confused. His face twisted in thought wondering how the boy had recognized him with the hood he was wearing.

"Go boy get out of here, this doesn't concern you. Go back and tend to your crops."

He turned away from the boy, and went back to focusing on his victim, who started to scream, "Negan you truly are a villain, stop this madness at once."

Negan was taking no quarter though as if some form of madness had come over the once very sane and colorful character.

"I'm afraid now that I've been made, I think I'll ru' off, and you can join me as my hostage, or maybe something more."

Whilst saying this Negan brought his knife to Madame Harron's small neck and she began to cry. The poor Madame Harron would gladly never find out what this mysterious fate meant, as at that moment the man received a punch in the jaw from the young, yet very muscular farm boy. He went backward and collapsed onto the remains of the cart; his blade went flying away from him in another direction. Herbert watched from the shadows of the destroyed cart, as Kregar stood over her, his arm still outstretched he had delivered the punch. He reached down and helped the poor assaulted woman to her feet.

"Thank you, Kregar, the fates bless you."

Kregar nodded, and had a bystander guide her away from the cart before turning to the dazed man who slowly began to rise.

"You know what boy," he began to say as he was getting to his feet.

"That was a good punch, too bad I won't let you do that again."

He was limping towards the blade, which was laying, on the ground in between the two of them, but Kregar was faster, and used his newfound energy and grabbed the blade before the oaf could, and held it up, the blade hanging in the crook's face.

"You need to pay for your crimes, Negan."

He moved the blade a few inches away, but in a no less threatening position.

"This isn't right. We are all poor, starving, and trying to get by."

He waved to the crowd who had just watched, awestruck by what was happening.

"Hurting people, destroying their property, forcing yourself onto them, that is not good people." Kregar carefully grabbed the blade, and with his strength he took the flat of the blade and broke it over a nearby cart, the blade made a metallic snap, and he threw it on the ground.

"Now you've been disarmed, and you're broken."

At that moment a bit of blood could be seen coming from the man's mouth where the punch was struck.

"You, what can you do, you're just a farm boy, with an attitude and no respect for his elders." Kregar smiled, and before Negan could react another punch had landed in his gut, and he went onto the ground on all fours.

"Your punishment should be death, but no I think you need to reflect on your crimes Negan, I Kregar, son of Dregar banish you from Buran, and subject you to live out the rest of your days as an outsider, and outlaw, may the fates grant you mercy you will find none here."

As though in a whirlwind of energy and excitement the crowd chanted echoing Kregar's words. "Banishment! Banishment!"

The call came from all around and the man who had been broken, was beaten. The crowd got closer and closer. Negan was trying to find an escape, after a moment, he found one and broke through the crowd and vanished off into the unknown, he was never seen in the city again.

The crowd seeing him depart was cheering and others clapped and shook hands with the young man who had saved a poor woman, some he scolded others he cheered with. Yet all in all it was a good day, after a short time a cart was seen being pulled into town and on it was his father and mother. They departed and approached their son, and without a word, they gave him a loving embrace. Herbert had moved into a nearby alleyway away from the crowds when a faint white light greeted him, it took the form of nothing, but Herbert knew who it was.

"So, you've chosen the boy?"

Herbert smiled and looked at the crowd of cheering people as they lifted Kregar off his feet and praised him.

"Yes, he's the one Istan; he will be our next king."

A moment went by as he watched them parade him down the street.

"Meet me on the hill in three days; I will crown him as the sun rises at midday."

The light faded, and altogether vanished. Herbert slowly went and joined in the festivities, and that night they met again in the barn. They were alone as Dregar, and his wife had long since gone to bed and all was quiet.

"So, what did this all mean?"

Kregar was asking him to recount all that had happened within the last day.

"Well, it means you can be king, you've proven your fair to those who are not of your kind; myself in this case. You looked out and aided one in need; like what happened at the market this day. All that is left is for you what do you want, Kregar?"

Kregar looked around him and looked up at the mouse.

"You do not jest about this, do you?"

Hebert shook his head, "I do not, if you want it, it is yours."

Kregar paced back and forth. "What if I refuse," he said with a slightly cocky smile. Herbert gave a moment of thought, "Well I would move on to the next and see, but that's what makes you special Kregar you are the first and I found you worthy. Just think about it, and if you will, we will be leaving in two days."

Kregar stood still when he mentioned the rate of haste he was given.

"Two days," Kregar looked up at the mouse who was giving him a look he might only describe as serious.

"Not two years, two months, or two weeks, two days."

The mouse nodded and was headed towards his hay bail.

"Yes, two days, so if you," he stopped looking down and saw that the boy was crying.

"I'll do it," he said, though his eyes were full of tears and his face was all scrunched up.

"I'll be your next king, but please I must have my goodbyes."

Herbert nodded, "And thus you shall have them my young friend, we will leave in two days. Make your goodbyes and pack your things, now I wish you a goodnight, and well rest. The next few days will be the hardest thus far."

Herbert vanished in the hay bales above, Kregar went back into the house and went to lay on his bed. His mind was fleeting with ideas, and fantasies. 'What was being a king like, what sort of power would he have,' the mind of the young man raced and went pacing back and forth thinking this and that, until he stopped. 'No,' he told himself.

"I cannot let being a king change who I am, I won't let it."

He went to sleep that night troubled, yet sure in mind. Outside his door, his father and mother had heard his outcry. They both looked at one another, and nodded; silently they both realized that he had made up his mind. They went back to bed, not wishing to wake up their son, knowing there was nothing they could do to change his set mind.

The next couple days' business was normal at the farmhouse, and many people from all around congratulated him on his bravery; others gave him and his family what gifts they could afford. Then at last, the faithful day came. They had to depart before dawn if they were to make it back to the capital by midday. Kregar and Herbert were outside the house saying their last goodbyes to their son, and the mouse.

"Be safe Kregar, and please try to visit," his father was saying as he handed him a pack and a sword they had lying around.

It was simple in nature, but a sound blade. It was very small in the large hands of Kregar. His mother hugged him for a fifth time, as she said her goodbyes.

"Don't get all crazy now you hear me young man. Behave yourself and be a good king."

She let him go and looked at the young mouse who was hanging out in a pocket on the young man's shirt.

"You'll watch after him won't you Herbert?"

The mouse nodded, "Of course my lady I shall keep an eye on him night and day. I shall give you, my word."

The woman nodded and walked behind her husband.

"You know if I had known a mouse was going to take my son away and make him a king, I would have thought I'd gone mad."

The farmer laughed at his little joke, and the couple went to the door and waved the pair off, the night was ending as they got on the main road and headed towards the capital. As the sun was reaching midmorning, a stir in the bushes altered the pair as a man in ragged clothes and a small dagger in hand came out and looked vengeful.

The man looked as though he hadn't eaten for a while, but Kregar and Herbert could tell immediately that this was Negan, the crook that had assaulted the woman at the market, the one they banished from the town.

"You little brat, you ruined me. I was having a good life swindling the poor and the desperate, but just had to ruin it all didn't you."

The knife jumped from one hand to the other.

"Well now I'm going to ruin you, I'll kill you, you stupid brat. You're dead."

He charged, the wild swinging of the blade causing him to miss Kregar entirely, and in response Kregar beat him down to the ground, with a swift kick in the gut, he was sure he broke a few bones in the process.

"You bastard, you'll pay for that." said the man struggling to get up as he found a blade on his throat.

"No, I won't, leave us be Negan, I don't need a broken man's blood on my hands."

Negan looked over the blade and was still in his hands.

"Sure, sure whatever you say right after you die!"

He came up suddenly and cut at the face of Kregar his cheek cut. For his part, Kregar grabbed Negan's arm and with the twist and thrust of the blade pierced his neck, making him gurgle with blood rushing out the wound and he bled out fast. Negan dropped to his hands, and blade dropped to the ground lost and forgotten. Kregar checked his cheek which Negan had slashed open. Herbert, who had been hiding inside the backpack of his friend, came out to see what had happened. When he did, he saw that Kegar was moving the body off the road and cleaning himself as best he could.

"Are you alright, Kregar," asked the mouse who looked over at his friend in a very concerned manner. Kregar looked down, his face a mixture of emotions.

"I let him live, Herbert, I gave him a second chance, and this is how he used it. What a waste." Herbert nodded, and watched as his friend carefully placed the body far from the road and into the woods.

"I cannot say what a man thinks, but I do know this, his judgment lies with the Fates now, and only they can decide what comes of him."

Kregar went back onto the path, and was making his way up the hill, when they saw it up in the far distance was the capital, but it was not how Herbert had seen just a handful of days prior, there were no people, but the city looked as though it had been repaired the smell of rot and decay did reach their noses. The castle, long since in disrepair, stood tall and glorious for all to see.

Herbert pointed to a hill nearby and said, "Go there, go to the top of the hill."

Kregar went that way, and once on top of the hill he set down his pack and sat on the rock. Herbert looked around, "Midday should be here shortly."

The mouse said judging by where the sun hung in the air.

After some time with the sun beating down on them, the mystery of the city's recovery came to them as a citizenry he had never seen before made their way out of the city and towards them on the hill. The first to be among them was an older man with graying hair. His clothing was white, and he carried a staff of the same color.

"Hail my lords," he said, coming closer to them.

Herbert came close and looked closely at the figure.

"Istan, is that you?"

The figure nodded, and looked over at the young man who didn't know what to do except watch. "Is he ready, Herbert?"

The mouse nodded, and in his own mouse way indicated that Kegar should come closer to the old man.

"Greetings Kregar, I am Istan are you ready for your coronation?"

Kregar didn't understand, "Coronation? What, coronation?"

Istan and Herbert smiled, "yours Kregar, you must be crowned in front of your people so they may see their new king."

The mouse was alight with joy. Kregar smiled and nodded. It was all he could manage.

"Yes," began Istan, "and what better way than in the company of other royals as well."

Herbert and Kregar looked at the figure with confusion.

"What other royals Istan?"

The mouse looked around. Istan in response guided their attention to streams of banners off in the distance flying towards them, so many there were looking at a field of color, but the grandest of them all was the very first. It was a simple banner with a large white face of a bagger with a crown above its head, and sword facing away from it making its center, amongst which was a field of green. There were others as well, one with many trees on a golden field. One that had a Mace in its center and one that had a horse on the field of gray. There were so many he and Herbert had never seen such a great host before. It was only a few mere moments before the host joined them. In their lead was a man that was roughly the age of Kregar's father. Yet he was much grander as he wore a fancy green tunic, and a grand silver crown. On his side was a sword that seemed dark with mystery. Yet he was merry as well as the rest of his party. By the time they arrived, several other common folks who had come from the city had joined them on the hill. Istan went in the middle and whispered a few words to the leader of the procession. The person nodded and said a few quiet words to his followers. Istan came back to Kregar and smiled.

"Your path has long been written to this moment, are you ready?"

Kregar looked down to Herbert who winked at the young man and nodded.

Kregar smiled, "I am ready."

Istan smiled, he extended his arms wide. While he gave his proud proclamation.

"Kneel, Kregar, son of Dregar."

Kregar knelt on the grassy hill and looked deep into the eyes of the ethereal being. He pulled out his sword, and with both his hands, he presented it to Istan.

"A family blade?"

Istan asked, curiously looking over the simple blade.

Kregar nodded, a sweltering of pride from deep within came out.

"Yes, it was my grandfathers during the war, and my father gave it to me."

Istan nodded and took the blade into his hands.

"With this blade, with these witnesses, and among this hill. I grant you Kregar no more, now King Kregar the Just, son of Dregar, King of Southan, Protector of the People, and Guardian of the South. Long may he reign."

The party of royal visitors and commonfolk chanted the last line, so it echoed across the hills. Istan had while he was making these titles brought the young king's sword to either side of his shoulders. Afterwards he handed the blade gently back to him, in which case he set aside, as he was Istan had produced a crown from his gown, and it stood a glimmering gold. It was encased with many rubies and other colorful gems. These encased the brim, and the towers of the grand design.

"Long live the new king."

Many bowed, others nodded in respect. As he approached the visitors, their leader finally spoke to him.

He nodded respectfully to King Kregar, "It is often said in my house in a strange country you find your closest friends, the hand of Than-In stands if you need our blades, we will come." Kregar nodded, "Southan would be honored to be friends with the kings of Than-In."

The two monarchs shook hands, and the crowd cheered, suddenly a voice called from the crowd. "Sirs, the feast is ready in the great hall!"

Everyone cheered, and slowly headed down the hill to the castle. Kregar and Gregory went down talking of kingly things, but Herbert had stayed on the hill with Istan and a man that was in the party with Gregory but had lingered. When Herbert turned, they were speaking together in a tongue he did not recognize.

"Istan, what now?"

The pair stopped and smiled at the mouse.

"Live my old friend, you have earned it."

The figure who was wearing blue robes nodded a humble grin upon his lips.

"Indeed, the world is filled with too much wickedness to take out the good."

Herbert looked down as the party was entering the city, it looked renewed. Herbert could not help but think of it as though from years past.

"What happened, how?"

The mouse was indicating to the city, and all that was done. That was when the blue one began to speak.

"Well I gathered all the loose commonfolk I could find and set them to the task, and with some of my magics we brought this city back to its former glory.'

Herbert smiled; indeed the city looked much as it had all those years before the decay. As he was looking out, a thought crossed his mind.

"Istan will it not be an issue that there are two kings?"

Istan looked lost, for merely a moment but quickly recovered.

"My dear friend, King Jenus passed away this morning. He is now in a better place. May his spirit rest in peace in the Halls of Mentros."

Herbert went over to the rock; he put his head in his hands and began to weep.

"I am sorry master I failed you, I promised I helped you, and I never did."

Istan patted his friend on the back, picked him up, and put him on the rock. Grabbing his chin made the mouse who was still crying look at him.

"Dry your eyes friend, he is at peace, one that he rightfully deserved, the elf had long addled his mind, it was a blessing he passed in peace."

Herbert wiped his eyes, but was still huffing, and grasping.

"Do not forget who he was, honor his memory, but death is a part of all paths, and we must accept this. Live for him and carry his name. Leave the dead, for they are gone, but never forget them, for they will never forget you."

Herbert nodded and tried to get a grip on himself.

"Come we must not let this day be mournful. The crowning of a king is a wondrous day."

As they began down the hill Herbert noticed that Istan wasn't with them, looking back he saw that he was vanishing.

"Istan, aren't you coming?"

The old man laughed, "I wish I could, but I have matters to attend to elsewhere, please drink a cup in my absence, I'll see you again soon."

With that, the old man known as the creator Istan vanished. He was not seen in that part of the world again, but some say that where he vanished white daisies grow ones that cannot die even in the grips of winter.

The blue stranger and Herbert went into the castle smiling.

"You know I have a wonderful stomach for a mouse."

Said Herbert when they spotted the barrels of wines and meads. The man in blue said in turn, "Well let's see what you can do against a wizard."

The pair laughed and began to drink the night away. That night there was much merriment and cheer. It seemed to have lasted for years, to some, but before the party was dismissed, King Keggar stood in front of his table, and made a toast to all saying, "I cannot be king without all of you, I thank all you my friends, allies, and people. May we live in peace once more!"

A cheer went up, and many drank. The king allowed the royal guests to stay as long as they required and allowed the common folk to drink and eat their fill.

The castle had not seen such activity in decades or longer. As the night finally drew to a close, and some had already departed, Herbert was in the kitchen drunkenly singing a song or another. As he did, he drank from a cup and collapsed onto the ground, he did not remember waking up, but when he opened his eyes, he saw a sight he would forever remember.

A corridor filled with white, there was no real color to be found, suddenly he saw materialize out of seemingly thin air, a man who wore grand robes, and a crown on his head. His hair was deep red, and his face young, but Herbert knew who it was instantly.

"Master," he called out to the figure.

King Jenus turned around and smiled, a laugh had left his lips as he called back.

"Herbert, come here you."

The king grabbed his pet and held him tight. Setting him in his palm, he had seen his true age. "Herbert, you've aged?"

Herbert was starting to cry, "Only waiting for you Jenus, I was waiting for you."

King Jenus set Herbert on his shoulder, and they walked off into the deeper light.

"I'm sorry my old friend we have so much to talk about."

The pair vanished into the light; they forever left this world, parting ways with it once and for all.

After some time, Kregar was looking for his elder mouse friend, he only found his body next to his cup, Ardon; the wizard in blue robes would later say that he died of old age, his soul had finally caught up with his body and had passed from this world.

After much delay, King Kregar was asked what his family sigil was, and immediately responded to the artisan, "A mouse, a gray house mouse."

The flag soon hung from all the flagpoles and banner mounts in the kingdom. The rains came back not only to the kingdom of Southon, but to all Mid-Gorthon. With this, the great drought finally ended, and the planting and harvesting seasons could carry on as before. One night many weeks later one of the castle servants who had been idle in their chores heard the king in the great hall of the castle whispering to one of the banners.

"They will know of your deeds old friend, I'm just honored to have known you, rest well Herbert savior of Southan, true protector of the realm."

Many years would pass, and the line of Kregars family would continue to rule, and everyone knew the story of Herbert the Mouse, passed down from parent to child till the end of their days.

The End

An Excerpt from M. J. Gusks Next Story --The War of Swords: A Legend of Gorthon

'I remember the late autumn breeze from that day. It was like any other, I was training my pupil in the courtyard. A smile on my face and a sword in my hand. Little did I know that that day would change everything.'

The young man felt the blow from the blunted sword hit him in the chest, knocking him back a few paces. Gregory had prepared to get hit but was still thrown off balance. Stumbling back into a defensive fighting stance, he tightened his grips. Breathing a little harder than before. His chest felt a new burning sensation. The training sword he used wiggled as his grip loosed, and he was nearly out of breath. He was losing strength and shaking; visibly he could feel it. His sword master looked at him with the mixed looks of a concerned mother, and a disappointed father. He had long brown hair, and long pointed ears; of course, he was an elf.

"Come now, your highness, this is the fifth time today, we can be here all day, but you're not leaving this courtyard until you can withstand my strike."

Yet the teacher was no ordinary elf; this was Lord Aradoth; sword master, teacher, friend, and not the least of which was the Lord Advisor to his father the king. Gregory heaved his sword forward, doing his best to control his breathing. Gregory knew in his armor he could take all the hits he needed, he told himself as he slowly approached the elf. He was in a low sword ready stance. His blade slightly to his left side.

Aradoth smiled, "You've tried this one before."

Warning his charge, reminding Gregory of earlier failures.

"I know, but this time I think I've got it." Gregory said with a bit more confidence than what he was feeling, he knew his stance couldn't hold against a determined attack, but he had a plan. "On-guard," shouted the elf as he dashed towards his student, and swung his sword to purposefully hit Gregory on his exposed right side.

However, Gregory feinted by stepping back, bringing his sword to a mid-guard position, and meeting the blade midair. The clang lasted a moment as he pushed the sword back, and he knew he had to time the strike precisely in the moment or he would fail. He swung his blade around and was coming in for the strike, but he was beaten and before he could bring the sword around his master's exposed right flank, there was a blade at his side, he felt the hit and collapsed onto the ground. A small groan left him as he lay there in pain. The hit wouldn't cause permanent damage to him, but it would leave a large bruise when they were done. As he looked up, he saw his master's sword in his face.

"Yield," Gregory put up his hands in response. Dropping his sword onto the ground.

"I gave you a chance," said the elf in a lecturing tone.

Aradoth put his sword in his sheath, and helped make sure his charge was still good to move, as he lifted him from the ground.

"Now what was the lesson we learned today?"

Gregory leaned stiffly over to his sword and picked it up, "Your sword lessons hurt."

He said in a slightly cocky attitude.

Aradoth clocked him upside the head, "No, it's called foolishness to outsmart the elf who's been training sword master's for over nine hundred years."

Gregory rubbed the back of his head, as he went to sit down on the bench nearby. Aradoth joined him and put his arm on Gregory's shoulders.

"I teach you these things because they will one day save your life. As I have all your forefathers for the last five-hundred years."

Removing his hand, they sat in silence for a few minutes watching a murder of crows fly into the nearby oak tree, as some leaves began to fall. Time seemed to stand still for a moment. As leaves hit the courtyard, Gregory asked, "What was my father like at my age?"

Aradoth was quiet for a moment and gave him a strange look. Gregory wondered what ideas and memories went through his mind. It seemed Aradoth wouldn't say a word.

When out of character a large and long laugh escaped from him, "Your father was the silliest of boys. He had lots of insecurities, and well he was not always so confident."

He breathed in deep as though thinking of moments from time long past.

"You're only worse in the sense of you having a big head."

The elf rubbed the long gold blonde hair of the prince and smiled.

"One day you'll take the throne, and your son will make those same silly memories."

Gregory nodded and smiled. He had a silent laugh thinking of all the trouble he caused and thought that in the past his father had probably done the same thing. He was never close to his father, but this made him almost relatable, Gregory let his mind wander.

The thought was not long as a large ginger bearded man came from the castle. His belly had a whole foot in front of him. This was Lord-General Ian Matthais; Commander of the Armies of Than-In. Yet for a large man he was racing like the wind for in a matter of seconds he was in front of the two, and out of breath. The large and very round face of the man was very sweaty. His beard covered up almost two/thirds of it. The rest were freckles and on his short stout nose, he had a pair of thin spectacles. His hair reached down to his shoulder and curled at the ends.

"My sirs, I'm sorry to interrupt your training session, but his majesty has called all council members to the war-chamber. Urgent news has just reached him, and demands all be present, you as well, young prince."

Gregory was shocked by the news; usually the council was only called as a ceremonial event or for times of great need. The last time this happened was when his grandfather King Justin fended off the Sea-Raiders in the south-west. That was over eighty years ago. He wondered what the cause could be this time.

"We shall make ourselves presentable; tell his majesty we will be with him shortly."

Aradoth stated bluntly, waving away the large man. Matthias gave each of them a bow, and made his way back to the castle in the same flurry of motion he had arrived in. Aradoth turned to Greory who looked confused by the sudden announcement.

"Come Gregory, we must make haste."

48

About the Author

M. J. Gusk was born in Minnesota. Is a first-time writer and is excited to share his work with the world. He spends his time writing or being with family. He enjoys traditional fantasy stories and a walk-through nature. He is currently hard at work with the rest of his fantasy settings and enjoying life to its fullest.

Printed in the United States
by Baker & Taylor Publisher Services